**Other Young Yearling Books
by Patricia Reilly Giff You Will Enjoy:**
(Illustrated by Blanche Sims)

THE NEW KIDS AT THE POLK STREET SCHOOL BOOKS:

WATCH OUT! MAN-EATING SNAKE
FANCY FEET
B-E-S-T FRIENDS
ALL ABOUT STACY
SPECTACULAR STONE SOUP
STACY SAYS GOOD-BYE

THE KIDS OF THE POLK STREET SCHOOL BOOKS:

LAZY LIONS, LUCKY LAMBS
SNAGGLE DOODLES
PURPLE CLIMBING DAYS
SAY "CHEESE"
SUNNY-SIDE UP
PICKLE PUSS *and more!*

YEARLING BOOKS/YOUNG YEARLINGS/YEARLING CLASSICS are designed especially to entertain and enlighten young people. Patricia Reilly Giff, consultant to this series, received the bachelor's degree from Marymount College. She holds the master's degree in history from St. John's University, and a Professional Diploma in Reading from Hofstra University. She was a teacher and reading consultant for many years, and is the author of numerous books for young readers.

For a complete listing of all Yearling titles, write to
Dell Readers Service, P.O. Box 1045,
South Holland, IL 60473.

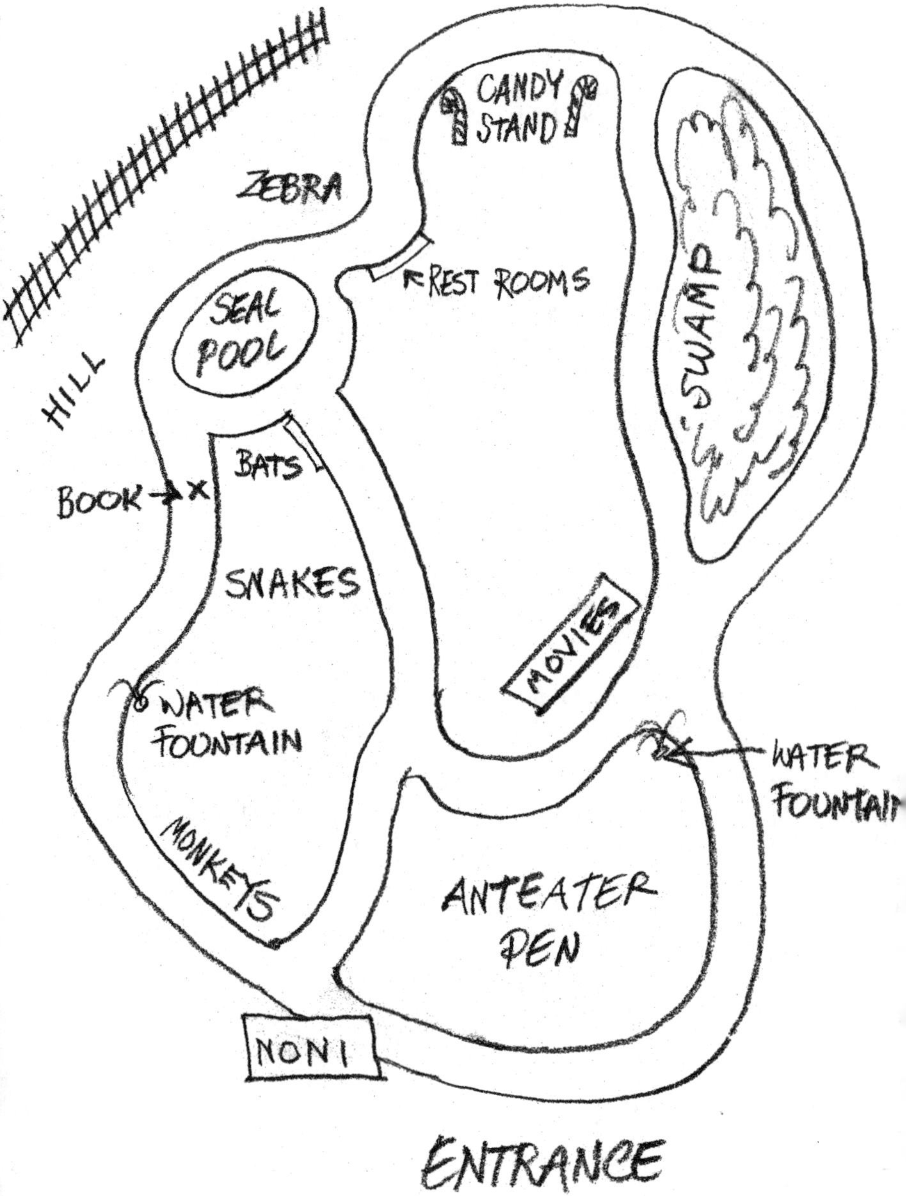
CANDY STAND
ZEBRA
REST ROOMS
SEAL POOL
HILL
SWAMP
BATS
BOOK
SNAKES
MOVIES
WATER FOUNTAIN
WATER FOUNTAIN
MONKEYS
ANTEATER PEN
NONI
ENTRANCE

THE POLKA DOT PRIVATE EYE

THE CLUE
AT THE ZOO

Patricia Reilly Giff

Illustrated by Blanche Sims

A YOUNG YEARLING BOOK

Published by
Dell Publishing
a division of
Bantam Doubleday Dell Publishing Group, Inc.
666 Fifth Avenue
New York, New York 10103

ISBN: 0-440-40318-9

Printed in the United States of America

August 1990

10 9 8 7 6 5 4 3 2 1

CWO

For my daughter,
Laurie,
with love

···CHAPTER ONE···

"What do you want to do today?" Dawn Bosco asked.

"I don't know." Jill Simon shook her head. The green plaid bows on her four braids shook too.

Dawn squinched her eyes almost shut. She peered out the screen door. "I have to find a mystery before school starts next week. Just one little—"

Dawn's grandmother put a bowl of grapes on the table. "I know what we're going to

1

do today," Noni said. She pointed to the street.

A car was stopping in front of the house.

Jill leaned forward. "Is that Arno? Arno Eliot and his mother?"

"I don't believe it," Dawn said. "What's that kid doing here?"

They had met Arno and his mother at the beach two weeks ago.

Noni and Mrs. Eliot were friends now.

Too bad.

Arno had to be the worst six-year-old kid in the world.

Dawn jammed her Polka Dot Private Eye hat down over her eyes.

She and Jill made gagging noises.

"Ssh," said Noni. "Here they come."

Arno was hopping up the path in front of his mother.

He had a yellow knapsack over his shoul-

ders. The straps were flying all over the place.

Arno had long skinny legs.

He had big fat knees.

He had a button that said:

I CAN SPELL . . . ALMOST.

Arno's mother looked worn out.

Anyone would be worn out if she had to take care of Arno, Dawn thought.

"Now, listen, girls," Noni whispered. "Don't make a fuss. Mrs. Eliot has to work. She needs a baby-sitter for Arno."

Dawn wiggled her nose. She made an anteater face. "I'm not going to baby-sit that—"

"Of course not," said Noni. "I am. I'm going to watch Arno all week." She smiled at Dawn. "And you can help."

Arno reached the top step.

He gave the screen door a kick.

4

"Open up," he yelled.

Dawn shuddered. She pushed open the door.

Behind Arno came Mrs. Eliot.

She was carrying about a hundred games and toys.

She dumped them on the floor. "Games that make you think," she said. "Arno always wins. He likes to think."

Dawn looked at one of the games.

She hoped she didn't have to play with him.

She didn't want to be beaten by a six-year-old boy.

"I like to spell too." Arno pointed at Dawn. "B-g n-s." He laughed. "Big nose."

"Almost right," said his mother. "Very good."

Dawn wiggled her nose again. She tried to make it look smaller.

Jill was grinning.

Arno pointed at Jill. "U-t-u," he said. "You too."

Dawn and Jill looked at each other. "Some kid," said Dawn.

"Bye, Arno," said his mother. She waved her hand.

She looked glad to go.

Arno didn't even notice she was leaving.

He was headed for the stairs.

"What's up there?" he asked.

"My bedroom," said Dawn. "It's private. Keep out."

Noni clicked her tongue at Dawn. "Let's be n-i-c-e," she spelled.

Arno looked back. "Let's be nuts?" he asked.

Dawn tried not to laugh.

She and Jill followed him up the stairs.

He stopped short at Dawn's bedroom door. "Just what I thought. Girl's stuff. Junk."

Dawn started to shut the door.

"Never mind," he said. "I'll take a look anyway."

"Look doesn't mean touch," she said.

Arno got down on the floor. His head disappeared under the bed . . . and then his shoulders.

"Get out of there," Dawn said.

He backed out again. "What's this?" He was dragging a polka dot box.

"It's a private eye box," said Dawn. "It has lots of stuff to solve crime."

Arno looked interested. He tried to open it.

"Locked," said Dawn. "The key is around my neck."

He held his hand out. "How about—"

"No." Dawn shook her head. She shoved the box under the bed again.

Arno stood up. "I bet you couldn't solve a crime."

"I solved one two weeks ago. Remember?"

"Bet a nickel you can't solve another one," said Arno.

"Don't bother."

"I'm rich," said Arno. "I can bet a dollar. Two dollars."

Dawn narrowed her eyes. "If I had a mystery to solve, I'd do it."

Arno didn't answer. He raced downstairs again.

"Can we go to the zoo?" he asked Noni.

Noni thought for a minute. "Why not?" she said.

"Good," said Arno. He stuck out his tongue at Dawn. "They'll probably put you in the alligator swamp."

Dawn gritted her teeth. "I'd like to put you in a lizard tank."

"I think we're ready to go," said Noni.

"Don't forget your private eye box," said Jill.

"You're right." Dawn started for the stairs.

With Arno around, there probably would be trouble.

···CHAPTER TWO···

Noni parked in the zoo lot. "Don't forget anything," she said.

Arno climbed out over Dawn.

His knapsack strap hit her in the nose.

"Ouch," Dawn said. "Why don't you close that thing?"

He crossed his eyes. "I'm going to look for alligators." He started across the lot.

Another car pulled in.

A woman got out with a dog.

She had a rose pinned to her hair.

So did the dog.

Dawn and Jill began to laugh.

The dog growled.

The girls ran to catch up with Arno.

"Wait," said Noni. She sank down on a bench under the trees. "My big toes are squished in these shoes. I think I'll sit here."

Dawn dropped her private eye box on the bench next to Noni. "Whew, that's heavy."

She opened it and grabbed her private eye hat. "I'll put this on, just in case."

"Let's go, let's go," said Arno. He ran halfway up the path, then back again. "Hurry."

Noni took a breath. "Tell you what. The three of you go together." She took out a crossword puzzle and a pencil. "You can leave your things here, Arno."

Arno thought about it.

He shook his head. "Someone might steal my stuff while you're not looking. My dollars too."

"Why don't you stay with Noni?" Dawn said. "You can watch everything yourself."

Noni lowered one eyebrow. She stared at Dawn.

"I guess not," Dawn said. She raised her shoulders in the air.

She and Jill started up the path.

Arno stopped to make faces at the monkeys. Then he dashed in front of them.

The path curved ahead of them.

Arno disappeared around the curve.

"Yeow," yelled a voice.

Dawn and Jill looked at each other. "What now?"

They raced to look.

A girl was rubbing her knee.

Two boys were sprawled on the ground. They looked like twins. Red balloons were tied to their wrists.

The woman with the rose was dashing up the path.

13

"Sorry." Arno raised his shoulders in the air. "Now I need a drink," he said.

He went back to the water fountain.

He straightened up. He looked at Dawn.

His cheeks were puffed with water.

"Don't try it," Dawn told him. "Don't even think about it."

Arno stared at her for another minute.

Then he spit the water onto a rosebush.

"Gross," said Jill.

"Double gross," said Dawn.

"Plants need water," said Arno.

He danced around them, then ran ahead again.

He kept yelling something back over his shoulder . . . something about alligators.

Dawn didn't pay attention.

She was looking for a mystery . . . looking hard.

At first everything seemed ordinary.

A green hill stretched up on one side of her. It was covered with shady trees.

On the other side was a stone house with a picture of a snake. Its tongue was darting out.

Dawn shivered a little.

She looked up the path toward the seal pool.

A seal with whiskers stared back at her.

Dawn smiled. Seals were fun.

"Hey," said Jill. "What's that?"

Dawn twirled around. A notebook was lying in the middle of the path.

"I don't think it was here a minute ago," Jill said. She bent down and picked it up.

Dawn looked over Jill's shoulder.

On the front, in yellow, it said:

FROM A TO Z

IT'S ME

Underneath, someone had written in crayon:

R.L.

Jill ran her fingers over the cover. "What's all this white stuff?"

She handed the book to Dawn.

Dawn could feel lumps stuck to the book. Small white lumps.

Jill opened to the first page.

There was no writing.

Just pictures . . . two of them.

"A red stop sign," said Dawn. "And a bottle."

"What does it mean?" Jill asked.

Dawn wrinkled her forehead. "The stop sign may mean *don't read*."

"What about the bottle?"

Dawn tried to think.

"There are letters on the bottle," Jill said.

"P-S-N," Dawn spelled out.

They looked at each other. "Poison," they said at the same time.

"The white lumps must be—" Dawn began.

Jill screeched. "Poison." She dropped the book on the ground.

They stood there staring.

Jill waved her hands in the air. "I've got this stuff all over me."

Dawn looked down at her own hands.

She could feel the gritty lumps under her fingernails.

Jill looked as if she were going to cry.

Jill cried a lot.

This time Dawn felt like crying too.

"I think we'd better wash our hands." She tried to sound calm.

Just then she thought of something else.

"Where's Arno?"

Jill was thinking the same thing. "What happened to that kid?"

Dawn spun around.

He was nowhere in sight.

They started to run.

Dawn poked her head into the snake house. A zillion snakes were slithering around in cages.

"Arno," she yelled.

The sound echoed through the room.

No one answered.

She raced up to the seal pool.

He wasn't there either.

She shaded her eyes and stared up the hill.

It was no use.

Arno was gone.

···CHAPTER THREE···

Dawn stood on tiptoes. She looked down the path. "What will Noni say? We have to find him."

Jill shook her head. "Not yet. We have to wash our hands. Right away. This minute."

"Wait. There's something else."

Dawn raced down the path. She looked for the book.

It was still there . . . right where Jill had dropped it.

She rubbed her hands on her jeans.

She had to solve the mystery, but she didn't want to touch the book.

She nudged it under a bush with her toe.

She'd find a way to look inside . . . after they washed their hands . . . after they found Arno.

"The girls' room is over here," Jill said. She held her hands out in front of her.

Dawn held her hands out too. She followed Jill inside.

She let the water run over her fingers for a long time.

Then she picked up a sliver of soap and began to scrub.

The door banged open.

A girl with a mud spot on her jeans was standing there . . . the girl who had been on the path.

The girl reached for a paper towel. She dabbed at her knee.

"Look at that," she said. "Some kid knocked me over a few minutes ago."

Dawn raised one eyebrow at Jill. "Arno." She reached for a towel too. "Did you see where he went?"

The girl pointed. "Toward the alligator swamp. Horrible place. I hope he found it. I hope they chomped his head right off."

Dawn's eyes widened. "Well, I don't hope that. Noni would—" She broke off. "Where's the alligator swamp?"

"I'll show you." The girl stuck out her hand. "My name is Candy." She grinned. "That's because I love you-know-what."

She raced ahead of them . . . past the seal pool . . . past the zebra's den.

Suddenly she stopped.

Dawn bumped into her.

Jill bumped into Dawn.

"What's the matter?" Dawn asked.

23

"I have to close my eyes as we go around the cotton-candy stand," she said. "Otherwise I'll have to stop for some."

They went around the stand, Candy looking in the opposite direction.

"I don't want to worry you," she said. "But all that kid has to do is jump over the rocks, climb the iron bars, and . . ."

Dawn ran her tongue over her lips. "He's too smart to walk into an alligator swamp."

"Some other kid thought he was smart too." Candy rubbed her nose. "Squish."

Dawn looked at Jill.

Jill's face was turning green . . . green as her bows.

"Don't worry," said Dawn. "She doesn't mean it."

"She's right," Candy said, winking.

"There it is," Dawn said. "I see it." She

pointed to a bunch of rocks and an iron fence with sharp points on top.

She took another look. In the center was a small pond in a circle of mud.

Brown alligators were lying half in the water, half in the mud.

One raised its head to look at her.

Dawn shivered. "We'd better find Arno right now."

"Right." Candy stopped and slapped her forehead. "Hey. I've got to go back. I think I lost . . ." She dashed off down the path.

"Your book?" Dawn asked.

"A to Z?" Jill asked at the same time. "Initials R.L.?"

It was too late.

Candy was running past the zebras.

"Come back," Dawn yelled. "We know where . . ."

The girl waved her hand. She disappeared around the path.

"Should we go after her?" Jill asked.

Dawn sighed. The mystery of the A-to-Z book had been solved too fast. "I think we'd better go after Arno first."

"I'll go this way," Jill said. "Straight around the swamp."

"Good," said Dawn. "I'll go the other way. We'll meet in the middle."

···CHAPTER FOUR···

Dawn started around her side of the swamp.

Ahead of her she could hear a roar.

It sounded like a lion . . . or maybe it was Arno.

She started to run.

A moment later, she bumped into something.

"Oof."

"Arno?" said a voice.

It was Jill.

"No, me," Dawn said as soon as she could talk.

"I heard—" Jill began.

"Me too," said Dawn.

Just then something dashed past them.

"Arno," yelled Dawn. "Arno Eliot."

"Can't stop," he yelled. His yellow knapsack bounced against his shoulders. "I'm looking for Fred's mother."

"Who's Fred?" Dawn yelled after him.

"It's a mystery," Arnold yelled back.

"We're supposed to be watching you. . . ." Dawn began.

But Arno had run around the curve.

He was gone.

"This is ridiculous," Jill said. "Everyone's running away."

"Never mind that," Dawn said. "Did you hear what he said? He has a mystery. I'll bet it's better than ours."

"Mystery shmystery," said Jill. "I'm dying to see the anteaters."

"Why don't you go to the movies?" asked a voice behind them.

Dawn twirled around.

A woman was smiling at them. She was wearing a tan uniform.

"I love the movies—" Jill began.

"Especially mysteries," said Dawn.

"It's about alligators."

"I don't think we have time," said Dawn.

"I hate alligators," said Jill.

The woman waved a paper in the air. "This tells all about it."

Dawn took one of the papers.

Jill took another.

"And there's the movie house," said the woman.

Dawn saw a boy with a yellow knapsack. "Arno."

He was pulling open the door of the movie house.

Dawn grabbed Jill's arm. "There goes Arno."

"And Candy too," said Jill, pointing.

Dawn nodded at the woman. "We'll try the movies." She turned to Jill. "You go ahead. There's something I have to do."

Dawn rushed back along the path. It was a long run.

She looked under the bush for the A-to-Z-is-me book.

At first she thought it wasn't there.

Then she saw it.

She wrapped the movie paper around it.

She picked it up with two fingers.

She wasn't taking any chances with that poison.

She ran back to the movie house. It was cool inside. It was dark too.

She couldn't see Arno.

She couldn't see Candy either.

Jill was there, though. She was sitting near the back.

Dawn could see her green plaid bows.

Dawn tiptoed down the aisle. She slid into a seat next to Jill.

The A-to-Z book was still in her hand.

She leaned over and dropped it on the floor in front of her.

Then she sat back.

The cushions were scratchy on her legs.

She moved around trying to get comfortable.

A moment later, music blared. A picture of a fat alligator came on the screen.

Someone in front clapped.

"Yuck," said Jill. "Who'd clap for an alligator?"

"Arno, maybe," said Dawn.

She stood up to take a look.

"Will you sit still?" a woman in back of

them asked. "You've been wiggling around since you got here."

Dawn ducked down. "Sorry."

A voice was telling everyone about alligators. "The female lays her eggs in the grass," it said.

"I'm never going to take my shoes off again," said Jill.

"Ssh," said the woman in back of them.

"About fifty eggs are laid," said the voice. "The young alligators are about nine inches long when they hatch."

"I can't look anymore," said Dawn.

Just then a hand tapped her on the shoulder.

She jumped.

It was Candy, in the aisle. She had a bottle of soda in one hand. She had a chocolate bar in the other. "Want a sip?" she asked.

Dawn shook her head. "No, thanks. Too many bubbles."

"Good grief," said the woman behind them.

"I have your book," Dawn whispered. "The poison one."

The girl looked down at the book.

She dropped the bottle of soda on the floor.

Soda sprayed over the seat. It spilled onto the carpet.

"Get me out of here," Candy said. She began to scream.

···CHAPTER FIVE···

Dawn looked down.

Soda was running all over the floor.

The book was a soggy mess.

She wrapped the movie paper around it again, scooped it up, and dashed outside after Candy.

The woman with the rose in her hair was kneeling in front of a bush.

Dawn hoped she wasn't cutting any flowers. She'd be in a lot of trouble.

"Wait for me," Jill yelled.

They looked around. Candy wasn't in front of the movie house. She wasn't on the path either.

"Where did she go?" Dawn asked.

Jill's lip was quivering. "Don't worry about her," she said. "Worry about us."

Dawn glanced down at the book in her hand. The poison was soaking through the wet paper.

Detectives had to face danger, she thought.

That's what her detective book said.

That's what she was doing.

Maybe the soda had drowned the poison.

She spotted Candy. She was bent over a drinking fountain.

She was scooping water and splashing it over her feet.

At the same time she was hopping up and down.

"I've been poisoned," she yelled.

"Let's go," Dawn told Jill. "We've got to find out what's going on."

At that moment the door of the movie house burst open.

Something flashed by.

It crashed into the bushes.

Jill grabbed her arm. "What was that?"

Dawn looked back over her shoulder. "Something yellow. Arno?"

Jill raised her shoulders in the air. "I guess so."

"Never mind him now," Dawn said.

She raced over to Candy and grabbed her arm. "Stop jumping for a minute, will you?" she asked.

"Don't touch me," Candy said.

Dawn tried to be calm.

Detectives are always calm.

"Tell me about your book," she said. "Why is it poisoned?"

"*My* book?" Candy screeched. "*My* book?"

Dawn nodded. "Your book."

Candy backed away from her. "It's not mine. I never saw it before."

Dawn shook her head. "I don't understand." She blinked. "You said you lost—"

"My purse." Candy held it up. "I left it on a bench."

She took another quick step away from Dawn. "Don't come near me. Crazy kid. Trying to give me a poison book. Trying to poison me! I ought to call the police."

Dawn stood there looking as she dashed away. "Ridiculous," she said.

Then she grinned at Jill. "Good. The mystery's still not solved."

"Do you hear what I hear?" Jill asked. She looked as if she were going to cry.

Then Dawn heard it too.

Horrible noises. Grunts. Snuffles.

"What's that?"

"It sounds like an animal. A horrible . . ." Jill began.

They started to run.

They didn't stop until they had passed the snake house.

They stopped for a quick breath.

"Something's gotten loose," said Jill.

Dawn looked around.

People were wandering around all over the place.

No one else seemed to be worried.

"Maybe it was something in a cage," she said.

"Maybe it wasn't," said Jill.

"I think we should go sit with Noni," Dawn said. "Just in case. I think we should look at this book again too. We may find another clue."

Just then the woman with the rose raced by.

The rose had fallen down over her ear.

"Have you seen a boy?" Dawn began.

The woman shook her head. "Have you seen a dog?"

"No, sorry," said Dawn.

The woman turned the corner and disappeared.

···CHAPTER SIX···

"Arrrr-no," Dawn screamed at the top of her lungs. "It's lunchtime."

She waited a minute. "Arrrr-no Eliot."

Jill tapped her shoulder. "Even Noni's going to hear you screaming."

"That kid is the worst pest," said Dawn. "Too bad about him."

They went down the path.

Dawn carried the book with two fingers.

Noni was still sitting on the bench. She was bent over her crossword puzzle.

She looked up when she heard them.

Dawn and Jill sank down on the bench. Dawn dropped the book underneath it and wiped her hands. Then she took a breath.

Noni wasn't going to be happy when she heard Arno was missing.

"I have to tell you—" Dawn began.

"I have your favorite sandwiches," Noni said at the same time. "Peanut butter and jelly."

"Bll-ech," said a voice behind them.

"Arno," Dawn said.

He sat down on the end of the bench. "Sardine sandwiches are my favorite," he said.

"I think I'm going to be sick," said Jill.

Noni stood up and poured juice for everyone.

"Too bad it's not the red kind," said Arno. "I'm not too crazy about orange."

Dawn crossed her eyes. "I'm not too crazy about him either," she whispered to Jill.

She took a bite of the sandwich Noni gave her. "Deee-licious."

She leaned back against the bench and tried to think. How was she going to solve this mystery?

"I think I need some dessert now," Arno said.

Noni frowned. "You didn't eat much of your sandwich."

Arno shook his head. "I'm saving it for my friend Fred. You don't have any crackers, do you? Fred loves them."

Jill looked up. She had peanut butter all over her mouth. "Did he find his mother yet?"

"Nope," said Arno. "He's hanging around the alligator pool, waiting."

"I hope he doesn't go near—" Noni began.

"Don't worry," said Arno. "He's not as smart as I am . . . but he isn't that dumb."

Dawn finished the middle of her sandwich. She hated crusts. "What does he look like?"

"Fred?" Arno looked up in the air. "Brown hair. Runs around a lot. Kind of nasty till you get to know him."

Dawn rolled her eyes at Jill. "He's not the only nasty one," she said under her breath.

Arno reached into the picnic basket. "Bananas? For dessert? I don't even like bananas to begin with. I bet Fred will hate them."

He stood up, grabbed two, and stuck his sandwich in his pocket. "See you later."

"Whoa," said Noni. "Wait a minute. You have to stay with the girls."

Arno took a step. "I'm just going to the alligator swamp. It's safe as anything."

Noni closed her eyes. "It doesn't sound safe to me."

"It is," said Dawn. "Really. It has a high fence."

"Well . . ." Noni nodded.

Arno took off down the path.

"Now I can think," said Dawn.

She picked up the book. The only way to solve this mystery was to look inside.

That's what she had to do.

Poison or no poison.

"You don't have any gloves," she asked Noni, "do you?"

"Gloves?" said Noni. "It's eighty degrees in the shade. I'm dying of the heat. Why would I—"

"Never mind," said Dawn.

"I know what you're thinking," said Jill. "I know exactly . . ."

Dawn drew in her breath. She flipped the book open with one finger.

She looked at the stop sign and the P-S-N bottle for a moment.

Then she stared at the initials. R.L.

Dawn squinched her eyes together. "Maybe his name is Richard."

"Or Robert?" Jill twirled a braid with one finger.

"I went to school with a Ruth," said Noni. "She had yellow boots and a silver bracelet." She looked up at the trees. "What was her last name, anyway?"

"Yes. It could be a girl," said Jill. "Rachel."

"It could be anything," said Dawn. She bent over and flipped to the next page.

"What is that mess?" Jill asked. She looked over Dawn's shoulder.

"Two arrows," said Dawn. "Two thick

51

pieces of paper pasted in like boxes. Two D's."

She reached for her private eye box. She opened it and fished around for her magnifying glass. "Let me take a look. . . ." she began.

"Two of everything," said Jill.

Noni picked up her crossword puzzle. "Just like twins."

"And nothing else in the rest of the book," said Jill.

"Wait a minute," said Dawn. She dropped the magnifying glass back in the box. "I just thought of something."

···CHAPTER SEVEN···

Dawn and Jill hurried up the path.

"Stop at the alligator swamp," Noni called after them. "Make sure Arno's all right."

Dawn waved back. "Don't you see?" she asked Jill.

"No." Jill tossed her braids in the air.

"One," said Dawn. "No poison."

Jill stopped at a fountain for a quick drink. "How do you know?"

Dawn sighed. "I'm a detective. I figured it out. Those boxes. They were thick. Pasted on."

Jill raised one shoulder.

"Paste," said Dawn. "White paste. All those gritty little things . . ."

"They were paste?" Jill asked.

Dawn nodded. "Now we've got to look for something else."

"Arno."

Dawn stood on tiptoes. "I have to get up that hill across from the snake house. Then I'll be able to see—" She broke off. "No, not Arno."

They started up the hill.

"What are we looking for?" Jill asked.

A whistle blew.

It blew a second time.

Dawn turned around.

"Off the hill," said a voice.

It was the woman with the tan uniform. "You'll mess up the grass," she said.

"No, we won't," Dawn promised. "We'll

tiptoe. We have to look for balloons. Two of them. Red ones."

The woman looked up in the air. Then she nodded. "Go ahead."

Dawn led the way up the hill.

Jill puffed behind her. "I don't understand," she said. "I just don't—"

"Two boxes," said Dawn. "Two boys."

"Of course," Jill said. "Two boxes. Two boys." She shook her braids. "What does that mean?"

They reached the top of the hill.

Dawn shaded her eyes with one hand. "Now listen. First we were on the path. Then we found the book. Right?"

"I guess so."

"So who was on the path? Who could have dropped it?"

Jill pulled on her braid. "Candy."

"Yes."

"The woman with the dog and the rose in her hair."

"Yes."

Jill nodded. "And that's it."

Dawn shook her head. "No."

"You can't count us," said Jill.

"What about—" Dawn began.

Jill grabbed her arm. "You're right. There was somebody else. Two other people." She pointed. "And there they are."

Dawn looked across the zoo from the hill.

There was a crowd in front of a building.

Above the crowd two red balloons were floating along.

"Twins," said Jill. "Twins were on the path too."

"Good thinking," said Dawn. *About time,* she said to herself.

They raced down the hill, over the rocks, and back onto the path.

The balloons disappeared.

"Inside," said Dawn. "They've gone inside."

Dawn darted in between a group of people. "Bat house," she said.

"Not me," said Jill. "If you think I'm going near those bats, you're crazy."

Jill plunked herself down on a bench. "I'll wait right here."

Dawn took a breath.

She didn't think bats were so bad.

Not nearly as bad as snakes.

She opened the door to the bat house.

Inside, everything looked red.

"Special lights," said the guard. "Bats sleep in the daytime. With these lights, the bats think it's night. They stay awake so you can see them flying around."

Dawn nodded. She stopped to look at a few bats hanging upside down.

It almost looked as if one were winking at her.

She winked back, just in case.

Ahead of her, she saw the balloons.

Carrying them were the twins.

"Wait up," she yelled. Her voice echoed in the huge room. "I've found your book."

···CHAPTER EIGHT···

The boys turned together.

They looked mean.

Dawn held out the book. "Is this yours?"

Blue Eyes took the book. "What a piece of junk," he said.

He began to turn the pages.

He looked at the arrows and the two boxes.

He picked at one of the boxes. "Look," he said. "There's money underneath. A dollar."

"Look under the other box," said Brown Eyes.

"Wait a minute," Dawn said. She put out her hand. "That's not your book."

"Sure it is." Blue Eyes winked at his twin.

Dawn grabbed the book. She started to run. She darted around a bat case and out the door.

"Get her," shouted Brown Eyes.

Dawn raced up the hill.

Where was Jill?

Where was the woman in the tan uniform?

Dawn didn't see the rock in front of her.

She felt herself falling, rolling.

The book flew out of her hand.

"Grab it," yelled Blue Eyes.

"No you don't!" Jill yelled from somewhere.

Dawn reached out for something to slow her down.

Nothing was there, though.

Any minute she'd hit the iron fence at the bottom.

She saw things in a blur.

Something brown on the path. Green trees.

Someone was calling.

Then arms reached out for her.

"Are you all right?" a voice asked.

Dawn looked up. She saw the woman with a rose dangling from one ear. "It's you again," she said.

The woman pushed at the rose and smiled. "I remember you, too."

Jill slid to a stop next to them. "I've got the book," she yelled. "Don't worry."

Dawn sat up, rubbing her head. She could see the twins. They were racing away.

"Not their book," she said. "Definitely not their book."

"I didn't think so," said Jill.

"Are you all right?" said the woman.

"I guess so," Dawn said. She brushed off her knees. "I was trying to solve a mystery, but . . ."

The woman was looking around. "I can't imagine where that dog—" She broke off. "Glad you're all right." She started toward the bat house calling, "Fifi, come back."

Jill sank down next to Dawn. "I'm worn out. All this running. Up and down. Back and forth. I haven't even seen one anteater."

"I know." Dawn sighed.

Then she sat up straight. "Just a minute. I just thought of something."

Jill sighed too. "I wish you wouldn't think. I wish you'd just forget about this whole thing."

"R.L.," said Dawn. "RRRRRR. LLLL-LLL. And P-S-N."

"And ABCDEF," said Jill.

"Don't be silly." Dawn tapped Jill on the shoulder. "I think I just solved the mystery."

"Good," said Jill. "Now how about going to see the anteaters?"

Dawn shook her head. "No. Just follow me."

They started up the path.

They passed the seal pool.

"Will you please tell me what's going on?" Jill asked.

"I'll show you," Dawn said. "In about half a minute."

···CHAPTER NINE···

A crowd was standing at the alligator swamp.

They were listening to a man in boots. "See its eyes," he was saying. "They're set on top of the alligator's head. That way the alligator can hide in the water. It still sees what's going on."

Dawn looked around.

Arno was standing on top of a rock. He had his arm around a large tan dog.

"Come on, Jill," Dawn whispered.

They tiptoed up behind Arno.

Dawn grabbed his shoulder. "Gotcha!"

Arno jumped.

The dog started to growl.

"You didn't scare me," said Arno. "Not one bit."

"Hey," said Jill. "That dog's a monster."

Dawn narrowed her eyes. "Sounds like the growling we heard before."

"I know," Arno began. "Remember I told you he was—"

"Alligators have short legs," said the man in boots. "They don't use them in the water, but it means they can walk in the swamp too."

"You owe me two dollars, Arno," said Dawn.

"These kids never keep quiet," said someone. It was the woman from the movie.

"Sorry," said Dawn. "Let's go somewhere else."

They wandered back onto the path.

"Two dollars," Dawn said again.

Arno shook his head. "Do not."

"You most certainly do," said Dawn. "I won the bet. I solved the mystery."

Arno ran his tongue around his lips. "You couldn't solve—"

"I have your book," said Dawn.

Arno looked surprised. "You figured that out? Not bad."

Jill looked surprised too. "Arno's book? Arno's? But his initials aren't R.L. They're A.E."

Arno shook his head. "Uh-uh. R.L. Listen. RRRRRRR-no. LLLLLLL-iot. That's my name."

Jill looked up at the sky. "Can't spell."

"I can almost," said Arno. He looked at Dawn. "How did you find out it was mine?"

"You dropped it on the path. On purpose." Dawn narrowed her eyes.

Arno was laughing.

She nodded. "It had to be you. I should have known it all along. It wasn't Candy. It wasn't the twins. It certainly wasn't the woman with the rose."

"Very good," said Arno.

"You hid your money in the book," said Dawn. "Then you wrote P-S-N on it for poison."

"You're going to take my dollars?" said Arno. "I'm just a poor little six-year-old kid and you're going to take my money."

Dawn narrowed her eyes. "I should dump you right in the alligator—"

Jill shivered. "Don't even think of that."

Dawn grinned. "Only kidding." She handed the book to Arno. "I should take your money. Instead I want to hear what a great detective I am."

"Well," Arno began. "I guess—"

"Yeow," Jill yelled. "I just solved a mystery. All by myself." She jumped up and down.

The dog began to growl.

Dawn and Arno looked at Jill. "You couldn't solve a mystery," said Arno.

That was just what Dawn was thinking.

She wouldn't say that, though.

Jill was a good friend.

Jill put her hands on her hips. "Where's Fred?" she asked Arno.

"That's right," said Dawn. "What happened to Fred?"

Arno pointed.

Jill pointed too. "I knew it," she said.

Dawn scratched her head. "The dog? The dog is Fred?"

"Right," said Arno. "I told you. FAT.

Fred's been running around all day looking for his mother."

"Wrong name," said Jill.

Dawn leaned over. She looked at the dog's collar. "F-I-F-I," she spelled. "Fifi."

"That spells Fifi?" said Arno. "I thought it was Fred."

"See what I mean?" said Jill. "The dog is Fifi. And the woman with the rose is looking all over for her."

Dawn slapped her head. "Very good, Jill. Very, very good."

Arno spoke up. "Fred had a rose in his hair too. It fell out."

Dawn and Jill nodded at each other. "You knocked everyone over," Dawn told him. "The woman must have dropped the leash . . ."

"And she's been looking for Fifi ever since," said Jill.

"Fred's mother," said Arno.

"Fifi's mother," said Jill.

"I can't believe it," said Arno. "You solved a mystery too."

Jill pulled at one braid. "Lost my bow somewhere."

"Never mind," said Dawn. "We'll find it. We've straightened everything else out. We just have to give the dog back to the woman with the rose, find your bow"—she grinned—"and then go see the anteaters."